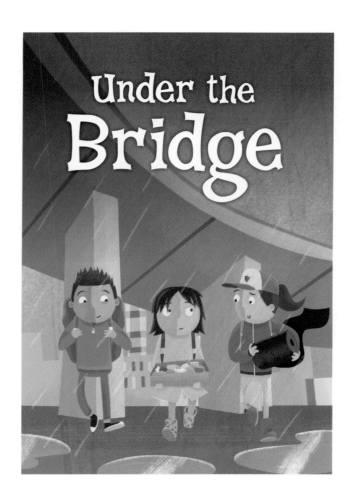

Under the Bridge

By Antonio Sacre, M.A.
Illustrated by Duncan Beedie

Publishing Credits

Rachelle Cracchiolo, M.S.Ed., *Publisher*
Conni Medina, M.A.Ed., *Editor in Chief*
Nika Fabienke, Ed.D., *Content Director*
Véronique Bos, *Creative Director*
Shaun N. Bernadou, *Art Director*
Seth Rogers, *Editor*
Valerie Morales, *Associate Editor*
Kevin Pham, *Graphic Designer*

Image Credits

Illustrated by Duncan Beedie

Library of Congress Cataloging-in-Publication Data

Names: Sacre, Antonio, 1968- author. | Beedie, Duncan, illustrator.
Title: Under the bridge / by Antonio Sacre, M.A. ; illustrated by Duncan
 Beedie.
Description: Huntington Beach, CA : Teacher Created Materials, [2020] |
 Includes book club questions. | Audience: Age 13. | Audience: Grades
 4-6. | Summary: "When a rainstorm in normally sunny Los Angeles adds a
 bit of fun to their day, Nina, Maricela, and Alejandro react in bold and
 brave ways to their fifth-grade teacher's comment about people who can't
 find shelter. They make a surprising discovery that shakes them to their
 core and propels them to look at their own world in a different way"--
 Provided by publisher.
Identifiers: LCCN 2019031463 (print) | LCCN 2019031464 (ebook) | ISBN
 9781644913543 (paperback) | ISBN 9781644914441 (ebook)
Subjects: LCSH: Readers (Elementary) | Homeless persons--Juvenile fiction.
Classification: LCC PE1119 .S167 2020 (print) | LCC PE1119 (ebook) | DDC
 428.6/2--dc23
LC record available at https://lccn.loc.gov/2019031463
LC ebook record available at https://lccn.loc.gov/2019031464

TCM | Teacher Created Materials

5301 Oceanus Drive
Huntington Beach, CA 92649-1030
www.tcmpub.com

ISBN 978-1-6449-1354-3
© 2020 Teacher Created Materials, Inc.
Printed in China
Nordica.082019.CA21901551

Table of Contents

CHAPTER ONE

Singin' in the Rain

Nina sloshed her paisley rain boots in the stream that formed along the sidewalk on her way to school. She twirled her umbrella at a dainty angle and tried to sing the old-timey song her dad always sang on the rare occasions it rained—something about singing and dancing in the rain. Rain in Los

Angeles made palm trees dance, cactus plants shimmer, and her heart feel light and free.

At the crosswalk in front of her school, a swift-moving torrent hid the yellow and white safety markings on the pavement and propelled leaves and trash quickly along its path to the ocean. Why did people litter? More than once, she'd ridden a wave at the beach and ended up with a plastic bag clamped to her arm.

She measured the water with her eyes and looked at her boots. Were they high enough to prevent her socks from getting soaked? Definitely not. There was only one thing to do.

SPLASH! She leapt in with both feet, laughing.

"Nina, *¡la lluvia!*" Her best friend Maricela leapt into the stream next to her, splashing both of them. She always spoke Spanish to her, even if there were people around who didn't understand it.

"I see the rain. Do you see the

rain?" Nina always answered back in English. Her parents wanted her to speak perfect English without any accent at all. Besides, some things were easier to say in English.

They both stood in a stream in the middle of the street, water pouring into their boots. A car honked impatiently at the edge of the crosswalk, and Maricela leapt back in fake alarm, splashing Nina.

Nina screamed in mock protest, stomping to splash Maricela back. Both grabbed hands, twirled their umbrellas, and danced across the crosswalk.

Inside the slick vestibule, both girls squeezed out their socks into a garbage can, pulled out fresh socks from their backpacks, slipped back into their shoes, and walked to class.

"Hey, want to go roller skating Saturday?"

"¡Fantastico! I'll tell Alejandro," Nina said.

COMPOST

PITCH

RECYCLE

8

CHAPTER TWO

CPR

Nina sauntered into class, got out her journal and favorite pencils, and started sketching. Some students came in with breakfast from the cafeteria. She knew some really needed the food and others just wanted it. Nina's mom always had breakfast for her, and the food the school served didn't compare. Except

for the coffee cake: that was a pure
sugar delight.

Señor Esparza came in, shaking
out his umbrella and hanging it in
the corner. His sharp eyes scanned
the classroom, and his quick smile
brightened the room, even in the gloom
of the rain.

"*Buenos días*, fifth graders!"

"Good morning, Señor Esparza!" the
class sing-songed in unison.

"What time is it?"

"Time to get a watch!"
chirped Maricela.

"Maricela, that's five more years of detention for you. Class-class?"

"Yes-yes!"

"If we add five more years of detention for Maricela, how old will she be now when she gets out?"

Alejandro pulled out a long sheet of paper, scribbled at the bottom, and announced in mock horror, "She'll be 258 years old!"

The class laughed, and Mr. Esparza implored, "CPR: compost, pitch, or recycle your breakfast items, and then get out your journals. Five minutes free flow about the rain. Go, go, go!"

Nina finished quickly and closed her journal. "Mr. Esparza, I did my free flow with words and pictures, can I take the compost down?"

"*Claro*, of course."

She maneuvered the canisters out of the classroom and meandered down the hall.

In the cafeteria, she unloaded the leftover food into a black bin while Mr.

Perez, the head custodian, wrangled the canisters and griped, "Squandered food going to the compost pile roils my blood! Doesn't anyone like apples?"

"I guess not," said Nina.

"This upsets me. It's such a shame we can't give it to impoverished people, especially those who live in tents under the bridge by the highway."

"Why not?" Nina asked.

"The school says it's a liability. If someone got sick eating our donated food, we could get sued." He sighed, grabbed an apple, and took a bite. "An apple a day keeps the doctor away!"

Nina headed back to class. When she settled down in her seat, Mr. Esparza chirped, "Pair share! And no reading with someone you've already read with this week!"

Nina swiveled toward Alejandro and asked, "Me first?"

Alejandro said, "Sure." She opened her journal, and read.

The Rain

Streets washed clean
palm fronds shiver and drops
flop
on top
of my mop
of hair, while Maricela sings
La Lluvia,
rain in Spanish
syllables of my parent's language,
join the dance of language in my head.

The world breathes deep this
cleansing shower
yet
plastic ruins, never rots, and mocks
and I
reach into the cold running stream,
so that this one piece of trash
won't make its way to the sea
I throw the slimy mess into the can.
Can I do more?
Sure.
But now, it's time for science.

Nina closed her journal. Alejandro gave her a thumbs-up.

"Class-class!" Mr. Esparza barked.

"Yes-yes!" the class answered.

"Today's science lesson: if the rain created a stream of water two feet wide along the curb of the underpass, how long would it take the people living in the encampment under the freeway to get totally soaked by passing vehicles?"

"That's subversive, Mr. E!" Alejandro shouted.

CHAPTER THREE

The Bottomless Pit

Later at lunch, Maricela and Nina nudged their food around their trays while Alejandro ate heartily.

"That was a huge bummer," Maricela said.

"Yeah, imagine, you'll be 258 years old when you get out of detention!" Alejandro shoveled more pizza into his mouth.

"No, Bottomless Pit, the people getting soaked under the bridge!"

Nina watched as the kids threw untouched food into the compost bin. Her eyes lit up, and she slammed both her palms onto the table.

"If we get the apples and carrots and unopened sandwiches before they go into the compost bin, the school technically won't be involved. Then, we could bring it all down to the underpass after school!"

Maricela saw a thick plastic roll of black garbage bags and added, "Maybe Mr. Perez will give us some bags that we can make into temporary rain coats."

Alejandro held up a half-eaten slice of pizza and mumbled with his mouth still full, "We could give them the rest of this pizza?"

Maricela squealed, "EWWWW! We are not giving them the rest of your pizza!"

He shrugged and shoved the rest in

his mouth.

Nina stared at Alejandro. "You are disgusting."

He smiled back, bits of pizza stuck to his front teeth.

"I take that back," Nina said. "NOW you are disgusting."

Alejandro gulped down the last of his milk, and the three friends went to find Mr. Perez.

ଔ

Back in class, the students scribbled in their journals while Mr. Esparza quietly read at his desk. A tiny plastic cat timer on his desk let out a surprisingly loud "Meow," and most students put down their pens and shook out their hands.

"Mr. Kitty the Cat says it's time to stop our poetry writing. Instead of pair share today, do we have a brave soul that will volunteer to read to the whole class?"

The class froze, no one daring to meet Mr. Esparza's eyes.

"*Vamos*, let's go, somebody?"

Nothing.

"You know, when you get to junior high…" Mr. Esparza trailed off, and the class let out a collective groan.

Nina said, "Somebody volunteer so we don't hear this lecture again!"

Maricela raised her hand, and Mr. Esparza smiled. "Thank you for saving your fellow learners from the highly educated musings of a genius teacher. You may read."

She nervously stood at her desk and read.

A Seed

Imagine a seed
pressed into dirt and soil, remnants of the past
once a boulder, a mountain, an ancient fallen tree
turned into soil
add water, once a wave, a tide, a raging river, a snowflake,
to drop and seep and meet with the seed to bloom!
bloom into stalk and leaf and to drink in the sun
to turn into
food
food that nourishes and delights

A Seed

Imagine a seed
pressed into dirt and soil, remnants of
the past
once a boulder, a mountain, an ancient
fallen tree
turned into soil
add water, once a wave, a tide, a raging
river, a snowflake,
to drop and seep and meet with the
seed to bloom!
Bloom into stalk and leaf and to drink
in the sun
to turn into
food
food that nourishes and delights
food that my people drive up from the
country in rusty trucks
following the harvest
to gather in hot fields
so we can throw it away
to a compost pile
while under the pass,
we go hungry.

CHAPTER FOUR

Under the Bridge

After school, Maricela, Nina, and Alejandro congregated in the hallway. Their shoulders sagged under their bulging backpacks as they walked down the steps and onto the street in front of the school. Maricela struggled to carry a thick roll of black bags in her arms.

"Are we really doing this?"

she asked.

"Yes, we are," said Nina.

Alejandro said, "The underpass...the final frontier. To boldly go where no one has gone before."

The rain sprinkled down as they waited at the crosswalk for the light to change. Maricela took a bag, ripped off a bit from the middle and the corners, and slid it over her head like a poncho.

"*Voilà*! Instant rain protection!"

They walked past the *panadería* and El Siete Mares taco stand and watched the stream of traffic thundering over the bridge. They ducked down the next street and curved their way back toward the underpass. When they entered the gloomy light under the bridge, the sound of the cars and trucks overhead echoed against the huge cement slabs, making conversation pointless.

A lamp with no cord stood next to a sagging sofa, and three bicycle tires leaned against the cushions. The three friends stared at the tires, trying to decipher the meaning of their placement.

They carefully approached the overturned corrugated boxes and smudged tents that marked the center of the little village. A sodden jacket lay splayed out on a dirty blue tarp in front of a squalid square tent.

"Hello?" Nina called, her voice tiny against the reverberation of the cars.

"Hello!" yelled Maricela.

"Yo, look at that!" Alejandro pointed to a bright red backpack just beyond the tarp that had a majestic white wolf painted on the flap. "That looks like Dante's backpack!" He stepped toward the tarp and looked at it more thoroughly. "It can't be his!"

A voice from inside the tent said, "It is."

Alejandro jumped back so quickly he slammed into Maricela, who let out a little yelp. Dante emerged from the tent, his school shirt still tucked into his pants.

"What are you doing here, Dante?" Nina asked.

"Visiting my mom." He stared at them, his eyes hard. He waited as the bridge shook ferociously. When the truck passed, he wondered, "What are you doing here?"

Maricela peeled off her makeshift raincoat and held it out as she unzipped

her backpack. "We're delivering some homemade raincoats and some of the leftover food we repurposed from the lunch room."

Nina and Alejandro opened their bags, too, and the three stood there, looking at their classmate.

Dante stared back, his face inscrutable. Two cars above on the viaduct got into a honking match, and in the cacophony, he stepped toward his classmates and took the food and the roll of bags. He slipped them into the tent and whispered something indiscernible. He pivoted around and said, "You can't tell anyone about this."

Alejandro's right eyebrow arched above his dark eyes, a look of concern clouding his jovial face. He scrutinized his friend's countenance and asked, "Do you live here?"

"No, I live with my aunt. My mom stays here, for now. The snacks will be good for the crew when they get back from the food bank. Not everyone can make it over there, and with the rain and all, this will really help. Thanks. Anyway, you should go now, before it gets too crazy down here."

Not knowing what to say, the friends headed home. At the top of the street, with the underpass a few blocks behind them, Nina whirled around. She knew they had to do something, even though they were only fifth graders, but they could try. They had to try.

Nina looked at her friends. "Where does Mr. Esparza say we should go if we have a really big problem?"

"Detention?" Maricela joked.

"The bathroom?" Alejandro said.

"For real, fools!"

All three concluded, "The library."

ა

The next afternoon, when Mr. Esparza's timer cat meowed, three hands shot straight up into the air. "To my mortification, class, it seems that the three musketeers have spoiled my lecture for today. Alejandro, would you like to recite your poem to the class?"

The White Wolf

Trucks Roar
Cars honk
Sofas sag
Lightless lamps
have no chance against the gloom.

Tents bend
Tarps beckon
Tires sit
a white wolf howls at the moon

You can't tell anyone about this

Besides, who would believe it?
A visit to the underpass
and my clean pillow and soft bed
mean so much more to me now.

As Alejandro finished reading, he looked at Nina and Maricela, and they nodded their heads in support. Nina summoned all of her courage and stood up at her desk. "Mr. Esparza, the three of us have an idea for our fifth grade culmination service project."

CHAPTER FIVE

Small Steps

Later that month, the school held an assembly outside. After Principal Gomez finished her announcements, Mr. Esparza took the microphone. "The Three Musketeers have something special to explain!"

Just then, Maricela, Nina, and Alejandro skated in from three

different directions. With a big smile,
Mr. Esparza handed the microphone
to Nina. She grabbed it and shouted,
"Who loves to roller skate?"

Alejandro asked, "Who loves pizza?"

Maricela added, "Who likes to
help people?"

Nina explained, "We're holding
a skate-a-thon at the roller rink next
month. Pepe's Pizza is donating the
food! We're trying to help some people
who really need it."

Nina handed the microphone to
Maricela. "Donation bins will be
placed by the office. We'll collect
canned goods, clothing, and money."

Alejandro took the microphone and
said, "We'll make kits and take them to
the people who live under the bridge."

Nina proclaimed, "We can do this
together! If each of us brings one item
of clothing, one can or box of food, one
bottle of water, and one $10 bill, we'll
be able to help so many people. And
we'll have fun skating!"

ⱋ

The three friends walked down to the underpass, dragging huge suitcases on wheels behind them. The underpass was still gloomy, but less frightening.

Maricela walked to the tarp in front of the square tent and unzipped her suitcase. She called in, "*Hola, Señora Hernández.* It's just us. We got some baby powder this time."

They waited for a response, but none came. Nina and Alejandro unzipped their suitcases, too, and all three carefully laid out the kits. They zipped up their suitcases and headed out of the shadows. At the edge of the underpass, Nina glanced back over her shoulder to see a hand slide out of the tent, pull one of the kits inside, and shoot back out again, thumb sticking straight up in the air. Nina yelled over her shoulder, "You're welcome, Mrs. H!"

The trio paused to look back at the encampment once more and then headed home.

About Us

The Author
Antonio Sacre was born in Boston to a father from Cuba and an Irish-American mother. He grew up speaking Spanish and English and now tells stories and writes books about what it was like growing up in those two cultures. He frequently helps youth facing homelessness tell their own stories. He lives in Los Angeles with his wife, two children, and two cats. Yes, he's a cat guy.

The Illustrator
Duncan Beedie is a children's picture-book author and illustrator from Bristol, England. He has been drawing and doodling since childhood, sprawled out on his parents' living room floor with a crayon in hand (although he sits upright to draw these days). He lives with his wife, daughter, and their tirelessly playful springer spaniel, Ivor.